WIND IN THE WILLOWS

KENNETH GRAHAME

BOOKS

Editor: Heather Hammonds
Cover Illustration: Terry Riley, sga Illustration & Design
Illustrations: Terry Riley, sga Illustration & Design
Typesetting: Midland Typesetters

Wind in the Willows
First published in 2007 by
Budget Books Pty Ltd
45–55 Fairchild Street
Heatherton Victoria 3202 Australia

ISBN: 978 1 7418 1486 6

Printed & bound in India

The Author
Kenneth Grahame
(1859–1932)

Kenneth Grahame based *Wind in the Willows* on bedtime stories that he told his only son, Alastair. He never meant to publish them, but the book finally appeared in 1908. It was to become one of the great children's classics.

A.A. Milne, the author of *Winnie-the-Pooh*, turned the book into a very popular play, *Toad of Toad Hall*. Since then, popular movies and television series have been made starring the creatures of the Wild Wood.

Grahame was the son of a Scottish lawyer. He became a senior official in the Bank of England while developing his writing. His other books include two earlier stories of childhood, *The Golden Age* and *Dream Days*.

Contents

Contents

Chapter 1
Mole Meets Ratty

Mole had been working very hard all morning, spring-cleaning his little home; first with brooms and dusters, then on ladders, steps and chairs with a pail of whitewash. He worked away until he had dust in his throat and eyes, splashes of whitewash all over his black fur, and an aching back and weary arms.

It was small wonder, then, that he suddenly flung down his brush of the floor and said, "Bother! Oh, blow it! Hang spring-cleaning!" and bolted out of the house without even waiting to put on his coat.

He made for the steep little tunnel that led upwards and out of the ground. Very soon after, his snout popped out into the sunlight. He found himself rolling in the warm grass of a great meadow.

"Now this is fine," he said to himself. "Much better than spring-cleaning!"

Jumping off all his four legs at once, he

raced joyfully across the meadow, wallowing in the delight of spring. He had just reached a corner of the meadow when an elderly rabbit popped its head out of the hedge.

"Hold up there," said the rabbit. "It'll cost you sixpence for the privilege of using this private track by our home."

Mole stuck his nose in the air contemptuously, bowled the rabbit over and continued on his way. Hither and thither he ran, crossing other meadows, small woods and hedgerows. He quickly saw how busy nature and all its creatures were. Birds were building nests everywhere. The wildflowers were budding and the leaves on the trees were bursting out.

He felt a little guilty that he had left his spring-cleaning. But then he thought again. "No! I'll be an idle dog among all these busy creatures and plants."

Soon after, he came upon a big river. Never in his life had he seen a river before. It was all a-shake and a-shiver, glinting and gleaming in the sun. Mole was fascinated. He trotted beside the river for a while and then, a little tired, sat down on the bank and listened to the river chattering and babbling past him.

As Mole sat there, looking across the river, a

Mole Meets Ratty

Running joyfully across the meadow

dark hole on the opposite bank caught his eye. He immediately thought what a snug home it might make. Then something else caught his eye. Something had winked at him from inside that hole.

A little brown creature with long whiskers emerged from the hole. He had a serious round face, with small near ears and thick silky fur. It was the Water Rat!

The two animals stood and looked at each other cautiously. They had not met before.

"Hello, Mole," said the Water Rat.

"Hello, Rat," replied Mole.

"Would you liked to come over?" asked the other.

"It's all very well to ask me," said Mole, "but this is the first river I have ever seen. How can I come over?"

Rat said nothing but stooped down, unfastened a rope and hauled it in. From the reeds, a small blue boat emerged. He boarded the boat and rowed across. "Get in and I'll row you back," he said.

Rat held Mole's front paw to steady himself as he clambered aboard.

"Do you know," said Mole, as Rat rowed off back toward the opposite bank, "I have never

Mole Meets Ratty

It was the Water Rat!

been on one of these before. What a wonderful way to travel. What a wonderful day this is!"

"Believe me," said Rat, "there is nothing better than simply messing about in boats. You can't beat simply messing . . ."

The Water Rat suddenly stopped speaking as Mole cried out. "Look out ahead!"

It was too late. The boat struck the bank full tilt. The dreamer, the joyous oarsman, lay on his back at the bottom of the boat, his heels in the air.

That didn't stop the Rat talking. "No," he said, picking himself up again. "There is nothing as enjoyable as simply messing about in boats. Nothing seems really to matter. That's the charm of it. Whether you arrive at your destination or whether you reach somewhere else, or whether you never get anywhere at all, it doesn't matter. Look here – if you've really nothing else to do this morning, supposing we drop down the river together and make a day of it?"

Mole waggled his toes from sheer happiness. "What a day!" he said. "Let's start right away."

Chapter 2

Messing About on the River

"Hold on a minute," said Rat, before launching the boat on its river voyage.

He leapt ashore and climbed up to his hole in the riverbank. He reappeared a moment later with a large wicker luncheon basket.

"What's inside?" asked Mole, wriggling with curiosity.

"There's cold chicken," replied Rat, starting to row the boat away from the bank, "and cold ham, cold beef, pickled gherkin salad, French bread rolls, sandwiches, ginger beer, lemonade, soda water . . ."

"Oh, stop!" cried Mole in ecstasy. "This is too much."

"Do you really think so?" inquired Rat seriously. "It's only what I always take on these little excursions, and the other animals always say I'm a mean beast and cut myself short of food."

Mole didn't hear a word he said. He was completely absorbed in his new life, intoxicated with the sparkle and ripple of the water, the scents and the sounds and the sunlight. He trailed a paw in the water and dreamed. Water Rat, like the good fellow he was, rowed away and didn't disturb Mole's peace.

After about another half an hour, Rat spoke again. "I like your clothes awfully, old chap," he said. "I particularly like your black velvet suit. One day, when I can afford one, I shall buy one."

"I beg your pardon," said Mole, breaking out of his river daydreams. "You must think me very rude not talking to you. But this is all so new to me. I've never been on a river before."

"*The* river!" corrected Rat.

"And you really do live beside this river?" said Mole. "What a jolly life."

"Yes," said Rat. "I live by it and with it; and on it and in it. It's brother and sister to me, and aunt and uncle, too. It's food and drink. It's my world and I don't want any other. What this river hasn't got is not worth having, and what it doesn't know is not worth knowing.

"My goodness, what times the river and I have had together! Whether it is winter or summer, spring or autumn, it has always got its fun and excitement. When the river floods in

Mole trailed a paw in the water.

February, my cellars and basement are brimming with water and the brown floodwater runs past my best bedroom window. When it drops away again, it leaves mud on my windows that smells like plum cake."

Mole listened to every word before interrupting. "But doesn't it get a bit dull at times? Just you and the river, and no one else to pass the time of day with?"

"My dear Mole," Rat replied. "I mustn't be hard on you because you're new to this area and of course, you don't know. The riverbank is so crowded these days that many people are moving away altogether. Oh, it's not what it used to be at all. Otters, kingfishers, dabchicks and moorhens, and so on."

"And what's over there?" asked Mole, pointing to some woodland on one side of the river.

"That? Oh, that's just the Wild Wood," said Rat. "We Riverbankers don't go there very much."

"Do you mean," asked Mole, rather nervously, "that there are animals who aren't very nice, living there?"

"W...e...ll, let me see," said Rat. "The squirrels are all right. And the rabbits – some

"Oh that's just the Wild Wood."

of them are a mixed lot. And then there's Badger, of course. He lives right in the heart of it, and he wouldn't live anywhere else even if you paid him. Nobody interferes with him though. They'd better not."

"Why?" said Mole. "Why should anyone interfere with him?"

"Well, of course, there are others," said Rat. "Weasels, stoats, foxes and so on. They're all right in a way. I'm very good friends with them, pass the time of day with them when we meet and all that. But you can't trust them and that's a fact."

"And what lies beyond the Wild Wood?" asked Mole.

"The wide world, of course," said Rat. "And that's something that doesn't matter to you or me. I've never been there and I'm never going to, either. Now, get ready, just a little way off is a backwater. That's where we'll have lunch."

Rat brought the boat alongside the bank, and Mole took out the food and laid it out on a fine tablecloth. But before they had time to take a single bite, an otter hauled himself out of the water and came across.

"You greedy beggars," said Otter. "Why didn't you invite me to lunch, Ratty?"

"It's a private lunch for my new friend, Mr. Mole," said Rat, introducing Mole to the otter.

"Proud to meet you," said Otter. "Such a rumpus everywhere today. The whole world seems to be out on the river!"

Chapter 3
Disaster!

"Who's out on the river today?" Rat asked Otter, as they ate their lunch.

"Toad's out, for one," he replied. "He's out in his brand new boat – new clothes – new everything!"

"Once he used to sail," Rat said to Mole. "Then he took to a houseboat and we had to go and stay with him and pretend we liked it. He was going to spend the rest of his life in the houseboat. Now it's rowing. But it's always the same with Toad. He soon tires of everything new and starts on something fresh."

"Such a good fellow, though," said Otter. "But he can't keep his balance; especially in a boat."

Just then, Rat saw Toad. His new boat came into view on the river, rolling this way and that with the weight of its occupant.

"Toad'll be out of that boat soon," said Rat, "if he keeps on rolling like that."

They watched as Toad disappeared into the distance.

Disaster!

Toad disappeared into the distance.

"Well," said Rat, after they had finished eating and Otter had returned to the river. "I suppose we'd better start for home."

"Oh please, Ratty, let me row," said Mole.

Ratty shook his head and smiled. "Wait till you've had a few lessons," he said. "It's not as easy as it looks."

But Mole had become very jealous of Rat doing all the rowing. He jumped up and seized the oars so suddenly that Rat fell off his seat, and ended up with his legs in the air for the second time that day.

"Stop it!" cried Rat. "You can't do it! You'll have us over!"

Mole thought it was going to be so easy. Why, Rat had rowed without any trouble at all. But Rat had been rowing for a long time. Mole had never held an oar before. He pulled back the oars with a hopeful flourish.

The oars missed the surface of the water completely. He totally overbalanced and his legs went flying into the air. He found himself lying on top of Rat. Greatly alarmed, Mole grabbed for the side of the boat. Disaster! Splash! Over went the boat, and both Rat and Mole plunged into the water.

Oh my, how cold the water was! How bright

and welcome the sun looked as Mole rose spluttering and coughing to the surface. How black was the despair when he found himself sinking again! Then a firm paw gripped him by the back of his neck. It was Rat. And how he was laughing, as he propelled Mole to the shore.

When Rat had rubbed Mole down a bit and wrung some of the water out of him, he gave him some advice. "Now," he said, "trot up and down the path for a while, to dry out."

Oh my, how cold the water was!

"Ratty, my generous friend," said Mole as they rowed home later, beneath a setting sun, "I am very sorry for my foolish and ungrateful behavior. My heart quails at my disgraceful performance. You saved my life. Can you forgive me?"

"Of course, my boy," was the answer. "What's a little wet to a Water Rat? I'm more in the water than out of it most days. Don't think any more about it."

Rat invited Mole to come back to his house to stay for a while, and promised that one day he would teach his new friend to swim, and to row a boat.

When they got home, Rat make a bright fire in the parlor, planted Mole in a comfortable armchair and even fetched him a dressing gown and a pair of slippers to wear, while his own clothes dried. Then he told Mole thrilling river stories until it was supper time.

After supper, a terribly sleepy Mole went to bed. He laid his head on the pillow in great contentment when he saw that the river was lapping at the window beside the bed.

That day was only the first of many similar ones for Mole, each of them longer and more interesting as summer moved onward.

Disaster!

Mole soon learned to swim and to row. And he learned the magic of living by the river, and the joy of hearing the wind rushing through the willow trees that lined the riverbank.

Chapter 4
Toad Hall

"Ratty," said Mole one bright summer morning, "can I ask you a favor?"

Rat was sitting on the riverbank, singing a little song that he had composed himself. Since early morning he had been swimming in the river, enjoying the company of his friends the ducks.

And when the ducks stood on their heads to feed underwater, Rat would dive down too and tickle their necks, just under where their chins would be if ducks had chins, until they were forced to return to the surface.

Oh, it made them so angry that they shook their feathers at him! But it was all in good fun and eventually Rat left them to get on with his own business. And his business that day had been to write a song he called *Duck's Ditty*.

Toad Hall

All along the backwater,
Through the rushes tall,
Ducks are a-dabbling,
Up tails all!

Ducks' tails, drakes' tails,
Yellow feet a-quiver,
Yellow bills all out of sight,
Busy in the river.

Slushy green undergrowth,
Where the roach swim –
Here we keep our larder,
Cool and full and dim.

Everyone for what he likes!
We like to be,
Heads up, tails up,
Dabbling free.

High in the blue above
Swifts whirl and call –
We are down a-dabbling,
Up tails all!

Rat was singing a little song.

"I don't know that I think very much of that little song, Rat," said Mole.

"Nor do the ducks," replied Rat.

"Never mind the ducks," said Mole. "What I want to ask you is whether you'll take me to see Mr. Toad. I do so want to meet him."

"Why, certainly," said the good-natured Rat, jumping to his feet. "Get the boat out. We'll paddle up to see him at once. It's never the wrong time to call on Toad. Early or late, he's always the same fellow; always good-tempered, always glad to see you and always sorry when you go!"

"Toad must be a very nice animal," said Mole, getting into the boat.

"He is indeed the best of animals. So simple, so good-natured and so affectionate. Possibly he's not that clever, though we can't all be geniuses. And maybe he does boast too much and can be deceitful. But he has some great qualities, does Toady."

They set off and soon reached a bend in the river where Mole saw a large old house built of mellow red bricks. Well-kept laws rolled down to the water's edge.

"There's Toad Hall," said Rat. "Toad is rather rich. He has a banqueting hall, stables and a boathouse, you know. The actual house is one of the most splendid in the area, though we don't tell Toad that."

Mole put away the oars and the boat glided to a stop by the boathouse. It was full of several different boats, but none of them looked very used.

"Toady is tired of boating now," said Rat. "With all his money, he's probably taken up a new pastime. Come on! Let's go and find him."

Rat and Mole got out of the boat and walked across the flower-decked lawns to the hall. They soon found Toad. He was sitting in a wicker garden chair studying a map rather seriously.

"Hooray!" he cried when he saw them, not waiting to be introduced to Mole. "This is splendid!"

"Just relax a moment," said Rat, throwing himself into a comfortable chair. Mole found another one for himself. Then the two of them admired Toad Hall.

"Finest house on the river, isn't it." boasted Toad. "Finest house anywhere! But enough of that. You are the very two animals I wanted to see. I was just going to send a boat for you, Ratty, with strict orders for you to be brought back here immediately. You've got to help me. It's most important."

Toad Hall

Chapter 5
The Open Road

"Why do you need me?" asked Rat. "Do you want to go boating with me?"

"Oh, pooh to boating!" exclaimed Toad. "Silly, boyish amusement. I gave that up a long time ago. Sheer waste of time, that's what it is. No, I've discovered the real thing; the only genuine occupation of a lifetime. I propose to devote the rest of my life to it. Now follow me to the stable yard and you shall see what you shall see!"

Toad led the way and Rat and Mole soon saw Toad's secret – a new gypsy caravan, shining in its canary-yellow, green and red colors.

"There you are!" cried Toad. "There's a real life for you. The open road calls. We shall travel the dusty highways, the lonely heath and rolling downs. Here today, gone tomorrow; travel, change, excitement! And this is the finest gypsy caravan ever built. Come and have a look inside."

A new gypsy caravan

Inside were sleeping bunks, a little table, cooking stove, bookshelves, a bird cage and lots of pots and pans.

"All complete!" said Toad. "The cupboards are stocked with soda water, bacon, jam, writing paper and dominoes. I've forgotten nothing. You'll discover that for yourselves when we start this afternoon."

"I beg your pardon," said Rat, "but did I hear you say something about 'we' and 'start' and 'this afternoon'?"

"Now, Ratty," said Toad, "You know you've got to come. I can't possibly manage without you. So please don't argue. It's all settled. I want to show you the world!"

"I don't care," replied Rat. "I'm not coming. I'm going to stick to my old river, live in a hole and mess about in boats forever. What's more, Mole is going to stick to me, aren't you Mole."

"Of course I am," said Mole. "But, all the same, Toad's plans do sound rather fun."

Mole had already fallen in love with the idea of seeing the world from the gypsy caravan.

Rat saw what Mole was thinking. He hated disappointing people. "Okay," he said. "Live for others! That's my motto. We shall come with you, Toad."

In no time at all, Toad had harnessed his old gray horse to the caravan and they were off.

It was a golden afternoon. Birds called out, "Good day to you!" as they rolled along. Rabbits, sitting at their front doors in the hedgerows, held up their paws and said, "Oh my! Oh my! Oh my!"

Late in the evening, tired, happy and miles from home, they finally pulled up for the night. They turned the horse loose and ate supper by the caravan. Toad talked endlessly about where they might go next as the stars grew bigger in the sky. At last, they crept into their bunks.

"This is the real life," said Toad sleepily. "Who needs an old river?"

"I do," said Rat. "I think about it all the time."

The Mole reached out in the darkness, took hold of Rat's paw and squeezed it. "Never mind, Ratty," he whispered. "Shall we run away tomorrow morning and go back home to the river?"

"Thanks, Mole," replied Rat. "No, I'll see this out. I'll stick by Toad for the trip. It won't take long. He'll soon tire of his caravan."

Birds called out as they rolled along.

The Open Road

The next day, Toad was so deeply asleep that he couldn't be woken. So Rat and Mole did all the jobs. They lit the fire, saw to the horse, cleaned the previous night's plates, bought milk and eggs from the nearest village and prepared breakfast.

Toad finally woke up, ate his breakfast and watched the other two do all the washing up. Rat and Mole told him very firmly that he would have to do his fair share of the work in the days ahead. That was bad news for Toad. He fought hard to stay in bed in the mornings, but Rat and Mole hauled him out to do his chores.

The magic of life on the open road wasn't looking so magical for Toad! But worse was to come. One afternoon the old gray horse was daydreaming and didn't see a motor car approaching at great speed, as they crossed a busy road. At the last minute, the horse pulled violently to the right, to avoid the car.

There was a terrible crash as horse and caravan, and Toad, Rat and Mole, suddenly found themselves upside-down at the bottom of the ditch. The caravan, Toad's pride and joy, was a wreck!

Toad waved his fist at the fast disappearing car. "Road hog!" he cried.

The caravan was a wreck.

Rat and Mole decided that they would go to the nearest town and find a blacksmith to come and repair the caravan.

"Oh, don't bother," said Toad. "I've had enough of caravans now. I never want to see another one again. But I must thank you for coming with me. If you hadn't, I would never have discovered what a waste of time caravans are. I shall find a new toy to play with."

"Told you so," Rat whispered to Mole. "I knew it wouldn't be long before he got tired of his latest interest."

That evening the three of them reached a small town and took a train, which dropped them off near Toad Hall. The old gray horse came with them in the goods van.

With Toad safely in bed, Rat and Mole returned to their boat. They rowed home and, at a very late hour indeed, sat down to a fine supper in their own comfortable riverside parlor.

"Now this is the life," said Rat. "You can't beat the river."

A few days later Toad's new toy arrived – a large and very expensive motor car!

Chapter 6
Lost in the Wood

Mole had long wanted to meet Mr. Badger. He sounded such an important person. But whenever Mole mentioned the fact, the Water Rat would say, "It's all right, Badger will turn up some day or other. He's always turning up, and then I'll introduce you."

No sooner had he said the words than there was a rustle in the bushes and a stripy head appeared. It was Badger.

"Come and join us, Badger," called Rat.

But the creature quickly disappeared without a word. "Badger simply hates society," said Rat. "We won't see him again today."

"But couldn't you ask him to supper?" asked Mole.

"He wouldn't come," replied Water Rat. "Badger hates being social. He hates invitations to supper."

"Well then, suppose we call on him," said Mole.

Oh, I'm sure he wouldn't like that all," said Rat, quite alarmed. "He's so very shy. I've never called on him myself. Besides, the whole thing is quite out of the question because he lives in the middle of the Wild Wood."

"Are you scared of entering the Wild Wood?" asked Mole.

"Of course not," Rat replied sharply. "But it's a long way to go and we can't do it. We'll see him again. Just be patient."

But Badger wasn't to be seen again that summer, and soon winter had arrived.

Rat slept quite a lot during winter. Sometimes he got up to write some poetry. Sometimes there were visitors. But mostly Rat and Mole would spend the evenings sitting around the fire, remembering the adventures of summer.

However, Mole was determined to visit Badger. One afternoon he decided to set off by himself. The country was bare and cold. The wind was blowing and snow lay on the ground as he approached the Wild Wood.

There was nothing to frighten Mole when he first entered the wood. But then darkness began to settle over it. Now, eyes seemed to stare out at him from every bush.

"Come and join us, Badger."

Suddenly a rabbit rushed past him.

"Get out of here, you fool!" it cried. "The Wild Wood is full of dangerous stoats and weasels."

Now the whole wood seemed to be on the move, creatures running here and there, crying out in fear as darkness descended. Mole panicked and started running in all directions. He ran up against things, he fell over things and into things. At last, exhausted, he took refuge in the hollow of an old tree. As he lay there panting and trembling, he heard a whistling and the sound of scampering feet rushing by.

He was terrified, and at last understood why Rat had wanted to keep him away from the Wild Wood.

***

Rat had not missed Mole at all, as he dozed quietly in front of the fire, in his comfortable den. When he awoke he called out, "Moly!" several times and, on receiving no answer, got up and went into the hall. Mole's cap was missing from its peg. His boots were nowhere to be seen.

Rat left his house and saw muddy footprints

Suddenly a rabbit rushed past him.

in the snow. All of a sudden, he knew where Mole had gone. The prints led straight towards the Wild Wood.

Rat looked serious. Then he stepped back into his house, strapped a belt around his waist and shoved a couple of pistols into it. Then he took up a thick staff and set off at a smart pace for the Wild Wood.

Chapter 7

Rat to the Rescue

It was almost dark when Rat reached the edge of the wood. He plunged into it without hesitation, looking anxiously from side to side for any sign of his friend. Here and there, wicked little faces popped out of holes to see who was approaching. But they soon popped back again when they saw Rat, armed with pistols and staff.

Rat reached the other side of the wood without a sign of Mole. So now he started crisscrossing the whole wood, leaving the safety of the well-trampled footpaths.

"Moly! Moly! Where are you?" he called out. "Where are you? It's me . . . old Ratty."

"Is that really you, Ratty?" came a feeble voice from inside the hollow of the long-dead tree.

Rat crept into the hollow and there he found Mole, exhausted and still trembling. "Oh, Mole," he said, "I did warn you to keep

Rat to the Rescue

Rat crept into the hollow.

out of the wood. We Riverbankers never come here by ourselves. If we have to enter the wood, we come in pairs.

"Besides there are hundreds of things one has to know, things that we understand but which you, as yet, don't. I'm talking about pass-words and mysterious signs, special plants you must carry in your pocket, verses to repeat and tricks to practice.

"These things are all simple enough when you know them, but you have to learn them first, or else you'll find yourself in trouble in this wood. Of course, if you were Badger or Otter, it would be quite a different matter."

"Surely the brave Mr. Toad wouldn't mind coming here alone," said Mole.

"Old Toad," laughed Rat. "He wouldn't show his face alone here; not for a hatful of gold."

Mole was cheered by both the sound of Ratty's laughter and the sight of the pistols in his belt.

It was now so dark that they decided to stay the night in the hollow. The next morning it was snowing heavily. They set off home but quickly found themselves completely lost in the thick snow. They wandered about the whole day, until they were both exhausted and wet through.

"It will be dark again soon," said Rat. "We must hurry."

They hadn't gone very far when Mole tripped on something hard, and fell down. He had cut his leg.

"You don't seem to be having much luck," said Rat. "But I'll soon bandage you up.

He tied a handkerchief around the wound. Mole was very grateful.

Just then, Rat let out of a cry of joy. "I can see what you tripped up on," he said excitedly. "It's a doorstep!"

"A doorstep?" asked a puzzled Mole.

Rat started clearing away the snow with his paws. Yes! It was a doorstep.

Now they both started digging, and soon had dug through to a small door, painted in dark green. An iron bell-pull hung from it and below it was a small brass plate with two words engraved on it:

Mr. Badger

Mole fell backwards into the snow with sheer surprise and delight. They had stumbled on Badger's underground home. "Ratty," he

Clearing away the snow with his paws

cried, "you are a real wonder. You're so clever,
I think you'd find anything if you wanted. If
only I had your brains."

"Well stop chatting," said Rat. "Get up and
ring the bell."

Mole rang the bell and they waited
patiently, stamping their feet to keep warm. At
last, they heard the sound of very slow foot-
steps approaching.

Slowly the door opened an inch or so; just
enough to reveal a long snout and a pair of
sleepy, blinking eyes.

Chapter 8
Mr. Badger

"Now, the very next time this happens, I shall be exceedingly angry," said a gruff and suspicious voice from behind the door. "Who is it this time? Who is disturbing people on such a night? Speak up!"

"Oh, Badger," cried Ratty, "let us in, please! It's me, Water Rat, and my new friend Mole. We've lost our way in the snow."

"What? Ratty, my dear little man!" exclaimed a far kinder voice, as Badger emerged from behind the door. "Come along in, both of you, at once. Why, you must be freezing. Well I never. Lost in the snow! And in the Wild Wood, too. Now come in immediately!"

The two animals tumbled over each other in their eagerness to get inside, and heard the door shut behind them with great joy and relief.

Badger was wearing a long dressing gown and slippers. He carried a candlestick in his paws, and looked as though he had been on his way to bed when the doorbell rang.

He looked down on Rat and Mole in a friendly way and patted both their heads.

"This is not the sort of weather for small animals to be out in," he said. "But I've got a good fire going and there's plenty to eat. Come into the kitchen."

Rat and Mole followed Badger down a long passageway with several doors leading off it. Badger pushed one open and they found themselves in the kitchen. They were greeted by the glow and warmth of a large fire.

In front of the fire were three comfortable armchairs, and in the center of the room was a large table. And from the rafters in the roof hung hams, bundles of dried herbs, onions and baskets of eggs.

Badger went and fetched dressing gowns and slippers for his guests, so that their clothes could dry over the fire. Later, he served Rat and Mole with a splendid supper. After they had eaten, they sat in front of the fire and chatted.

"And what's the news from the riverbank?" asked Badger.

"Oh, much the same," replied Rat. "Toad ran off the road with his new motor car and now he's thinking of buying another one. Never was

"Come along in, both of you, at once."

there a worse driver than Toad! He's crashed seven cars. He's been in hospital three times."

"I'll tell you what, Ratty," said Badger. "When winter ends and the good weather returns, you, me and your friend Mole will take Toad in hand. We'll take no nonsense and we'll make him see sense. But now it's bedtime."

Badger led the two animals to an attic room with two beds in it. This was where Badger kept his winter stores. It was full of apples, turnips, pears, turnips, nuts, potatoes and jars of honey. Rat and Mole were soon asleep between lavender-scented sheets.

In the morning, the two friends came downstairs to find no sign of Badger. However, two small hedgehogs were seated at the breakfast table.

"And where have you come from?" asked Rat.

"Me and Billy were on our way to school this morning when we got lost in the snow," said one of the hedgehogs. "We stumbled on Mr. Badger's door and here we are. He's a kind-hearted gentleman, as everybody knows."

"And where's Mr. Badger?" asked Mole.

"He's gone to work in his study," said Billy. "And he doesn't want to be disturbed."

Asleep between lavender-scented sheets

Rat knew what that meant. Badgers always slept a lot in winter. No doubt Badger had put his feet up and was deeply asleep already.

All at once, the door bell rang. Mole went and answered it. It was Otter.

"We've all been searching for you," he said. "We found you'd gone missing. We should have guessed you would have been at Badger's. He's always rescuing someone or other."

And while Badger slept on in a deep sleep, Rat, Mole and Otter set off back to Rat's little house.

Chapter 9
Mole Goes Home

On the way back to Rat's house, Mole started to think about his old home. Since leaving on that bright spring day he had hardly given his own little house a single thought. Now all sorts of memories came rushing back. His home had been a happy one and now it seemed it was calling him back; it had missed him.

"Ratty! Hold on! Come back!" Mole called out to his friend, who was walking way ahead of him with Otter.

"Oh, come along Mole," said Rat. "We must hurry on. There's more snow on the way."

"Please stop, Ratty," pleaded Mole, after they had walked a little further. "You don't understand. It's my home; my old home. I can smell it. It's close by. I must go to it. I can feel it calling me. Please, Ratty, come back."

But now Rat was too far ahead to hear what Mole was saying. And Otter had left them, returning to the river.

Mole stood alone on the track, his heart torn between the call of his old home and his new

"Ratty! Hold on! Come back!"

friend ahead. But however strong the pull of his old home, he still felt he must follow Rat.

Running on, he soon caught up with Rat, who now began to chat happily about what they would do when they got back; how cheerful the logs of the fire would look and what a lovely supper they would have. Rat didn't notice how upset Mole was until his friend suddenly began to cry.

"What's the matter, old fellow?" asked Rat.

Poor Mole found it difficult to get the words out between his sobs. "I know it's just a shabby old place," he choked. "It's not like your comfortable house, nor like Toad Hall, or even like Badger's great house. But it was *my* little home. I was fond of it. But I left it and forgot all about it. And then I smelt it again. Oh how I wanted to go back to it! But I had to follow you."

"Oh dear," said Rat. "I understand. What a pig I have been! A pig – that's me!"

He waited until Mole's sobs had become quieter before speaking again. "We must go back. We must go and find that old home of yours. Come on!"

"Oh, it's too late now," said Mole. "Think

Mole suddenly began to cry.

about your lovely fire and fine supper awaiting us on the riverbank."

"Hang the riverbank!" replied Rat. "We must find your home. Take my arm, old chap."

So they set off, back along the track. The closer they got to Mole's old home, the faster he went. Now Mole had the scent strongly in his nose. They crossed a field and went under a hedgerow. The next thing Rat knew, Mole had vanished down a hole. Rat followed and found himself standing with Mole by a door. It was marked with a sign saying *Mole End.*

Mole went inside and lit a lamp. He saw that a thick layer of dust now covered everything in his old home. The whole place looked so neglected, shabby and sad.

"Oh, Ratty," he said, "why did I ever bring you to this poor, cold place on such a winter's night, especially when you could be sitting in front of your warm fire at home?"

Rat wasn't paying attention. He was running here and there, opening doors, inspecting cupboards and lighting lamps and candles.

"What a fine house this is," he announced. "So compact. So well planned. Everything in its place. We'll make a jolly night of it here. The first thing we want is a good fire. I'll see to that. I'll fetch the wood and coal, and I'll get a duster too."

Encouraged by Rat's excitement, Mole started to dust and polish everything. Soon his little home was clean once more, and Rat had got a cheerful blaze going in the fireplace.

Then Mole suddenly became sad again. "Rat," he said, "what about your supper? I've nothing to give you."

"Don't give up!" cried Rat. "I saw a sardine can opener in the kitchen, and every house always has a tin of sardines about. Come on! We'll find some."

Soon his little home was clean once more.

They searched the kitchen and eventually did find a tin of sardines, and a box of biscuits.

"Now there's a banquet for you," said Rat. "I know some animals that would give their ears to be sitting down to supper with us tonight."

"But we have no bread," said Mole, "and nothing to drink."

"Drink?" said Rat. "I saw a cellar door down the corridor. I'll look in there."

A moment later Rat returned with a large bottle of lemonade he had found. "Now we have everything," he said. "Oh, what a jolly place this is."

Just then the two of them heard the sounds of scuffling coming down the tunnel outside Mole's front door. Then came the sound of voices.

"Come along!" said one. "Now stand all in a line and clear all your throats. Billy, no coughing. Now after me, one, two three . . ."

Mole knew exactly who was outside. They came every year. Excitedly, he ran towards his front door. Rat quickly followed.

Chapter 10
Christmas Cheer

Mole opened his front door and there, in the flickering light of an old lantern, stood ten field mice. They had gathered in a semi-circle around Mole's door.

"What's this?" cried Rat, looking at the creatures, who were all wearing red scarves and stamping their feet to keep warm.

"I just remembered; it's Christmas Eve!" replied Mole. "Every year the field mice come carol-singing and they never forget to call on me. I always give them a drink, and supper too sometimes. It'll be like old times to hear them again."

Suddenly, one of the mice cried out, "One, two three!" and the carol-singing began.

Villagers all, this frosty tide,
Let your doors swing open wide,
Though wind may follow, and snow besides,
Yet draw us in by your fire to bide;
Joy shall be yours in the morning!

The carol-singing began.

Here we stand in the cold and the sleet,
Blowing fingers and stamping feet,
Come from far away you to greet,
You by the fire and we in the street;
Bidding you joy in the morning!

"Very well sung, boys" cried Rat when they finished. "And now you must come in, warm yourselves by the fire and have something to eat."

"Yes, indeed," said Mole eagerly. "This is just like old times. Shut the door after you. Pull the sofa up to the fire."

There wasn't much food to go around. But it was the happiest feast they had enjoyed for years. As they ate, they all talked about old times. The field mice gave Mole all the latest gossip. Rat said little, but just watched the happy scene and served the food.

Afterwards, the field mice acted out a play about pirates. Rat and Mole enjoyed it hugely.

It was late by the time the field mice finally left. When the door closed behind them, Mole and Rat poked the fire, drew up their chairs and had a last drink of lemonade as they discussed the events of the day.

At last, Rat, with a tremendous yawn, said,

Having a last drink of lemonade

"Mole, old chap, I'm almost asleep. I'm ready to drop. Can I sleep in one of your bunks tonight?"

"Of course," said Mole.

"You really do have a fine house here," said Rat. "I'd much rather sleep in a bunk than a bed. Much more fun. This is a wonderful house. Everything is so handy."

Rat clambered into his bunk and rolled himself up in the blankets. He was asleep in moments.

Mole was very weary too, what with all the excitement of the night and returning home. He climbed into his bunk, but he didn't go to sleep immediately. He lay on his back, his eyes wandering around the room. The old room appeared very mellow in the lamplight. All around him were familiar and friendly things which had long been a part of him.

Mole recognized how important all those things were. They gave him security and made him feel safe. He did not want to abandon his new life with friends like Rat. He knew that was where his life lay now.

Yet he promised himself that he would often come back in future, just to remind himself of how important his old home had been and still was. Forever after, it would be good to think he could return whenever he wanted; and the house would always give him the same happy welcome.

Mole slept in deep peace that night. It was late on Christmas morning when he and Rat finally awoke.

"A Happy Christmas to you, Ratty," said Mole.

"And to you, my dear old friend," replied Rat.

"And to you, my dear old house too," added Mole.

Chapter 11
A Sensible Toad

Winter turned to spring and soon it was summer once more on the riverbank. One morning, Mr. Badger arrived at Rat's house.

"The hour has come," he announced.

"What hour?" asked Rat.

"Toad's hour, of course," said Badger. "I said that when winter ended I would take him in hand and get him sorted out. Well, the hour has come."

"Hooray!" said Mole. "We'll teach him to be a sensible Toad."

"I learnt last night," said Badger, "that Toad had just taken delivery of another new and exceptionally powerful motor car. It has already arrived at Toad Hall. Who knows what damage he might do to himself or others with that speedy new vehicle. We must act before it is too late. And you two must accompany me."

"Right you are," agreed Rat. "We'll teach him to be sensible. He mustn't be allowed to become the terror of the highways."

And so they set off on their important mission.

They reached Toad Hall and spotted the shiny new motor car standing at the front of the house. As they walked up the driveway, the door of the house was flung open. Toad, wearing goggles, cap, an enormous overcoat and driving gloves, came swaggering down the steps.

"Hello! Hello, my friends," he said, cheerfully. "You're just in time to come for a drive."

"No," said Badger, "we're just in time *not* to go for a drive. Now come along."

With that, Badger, Rat and Mole suddenly lifted Toad up and hauled him back into the house.

"Now the first thing is to get those stupid clothes off," said Badger. "Come on Toad, take them off."

"Shan't!" Toad replied sharply. "What's the meaning of all this?"

There was no answer as Badger, Rat and Mole removed his motoring clothes.

At last Toad was just Toad again, and no longer a threat to everyone on the high road.

"Now listen to me," said Badger severely.

Toad came swaggering down the steps.

A Sensible Toad

"You knew it would come to this eventually. You've disregarded all our warnings. You are still wasting all the money that your father left you. And you're getting us animals a bad name by your furious driving and your motor car crashes.

"We let you get away with it for a while, but we animals never allow our friends to make fools of themselves. Now, you're a good fellow in many respects and we don't want to be too hard on you. Follow me to the drawing room and there you will hear some facts about yourself. Then we'll see if you come out of that room the same Toad that went in."

Badger took Toad firmly by the arm and led him into the drawing room. He closed the door behind them. Rat and Mole made themselves comfortable in two of Toad's best armchairs. Through the door, they could hear the drone of Badger's voice as he lectured Toad on his behavior.

It was some time before Badger and Toad emerged.

"I am glad to announce," said Badger, "that Toad has at last seen the error of his ways. He is sorry for his misconduct in the past and has solemnly promised to give up motor cars forever."

Badger led Toad into the drawing room.

A Sensible Toad

"That is very good news," said Rat, "if only . . . if only he keeps his promise."

Rat knew Toad could forget promises as easily as he made them.

"Right, Toad," said Badger. "Now you must promise Mole and Rat what you have just promised me. First, tell them that you are sorry for all that you have done and you've seen the folly of your ways." . . .

Toad looked sulkily at his friends. "No!" he said. "I'm not sorry. I haven't seen the folly of my ways. It was simply glorious. I love cars and I love speed. I shall drive as fast and furiously as I like."

Badger was very angry. "But you promised me in the drawing room!" he said.

"Oh yes," Toad replied. "I'd have said anything in there. You're so eloquent, Badger; so persuasive and convincing. But out here again, I find that I'm not really sorry at all. And it's no earthly use in my saying so."

"So do you promise never to touch a motor car again?"

"Certainly not!" said Toad. "In fact, I faithfully promise that the very first motor car I see, I shall jump straight in and off I'll go!"

Chapter 12
Toad Goes to Jail

"Right, Toad!" said Badger. "If you refuse to give up driving, then you'll have to be locked in your bedroom until you promise us that you will. We'll take it in turns to guard you. And your new car will be sent back to where it came from."

"It's for your own good, Toady," said Rat, escorting the prisoner to his bedroom. "Besides, we'll have such fun playing games together, even if you are our prisoner. And when you finally promise us that you'll give up motor cars, you'll be richer than ever. We'll have saved you spending so much money."

Now Toad was a wily old creature. He played along with his captors' game for a few days but at the first chance, he made his escape out of his bedroom window and down a drainpipe. He would have driven off in his new car if it had been there. But Badger had already returned it.

Toad made his escape down a drainpipe.

So Toad headed for the nearest village. He had just arrived when he saw a man park his car at the local inn. "There can't be any harm in just looking at it," he said to himself. "I'll only be looking."

Toad walked slowly up to the car and examined it in detail. "I wonder," he said, "if this kind of car starts as easily a mine used to."

The temptation was just too great. The next moment he was sitting in it; the next he had started the engine. Seconds later, he was driving away into the countryside. He increased his speed until he was racing down country lanes and out onto the open road.

He was so happy. He was Toad again! He was Toad at his best; Toad, the Terror of the roads; Toad, the driver that all other motorists must beware of. Faster, ever faster he went. Then disaster struck!

***

A few days later Toad found himself in court, charged with stealing a valuable car, driving it dangerously and crashing it into a ditch.

"What is the stiffest penalty we can impose?" asked the judge.

"What is the stiffest penalty we can impose?"

"A year in prison for stealing the car," said the court clerk. "Another three years for driving it fast and fifteen years for crashing it into a ditch."

"Nineteen years in all," said the judge.

"Better make it a round twenty years," said the clerk, "to be on the safe side."

"An excellent suggestion!" said the judge. Then he told the miserable prisoner to stand up. "I sentence you to twenty years in prison," he said.

The jailor dragged poor Toad in chains from the courthouse, and out into the street. The people outside the courthouse immediately decided he was a terrible criminal, and greeted him with jeers and hoots, and threw rotten carrots and tomatoes at him.

Laughing children followed him on his way across to the ancient castle, whose towers soared high above the town. Once inside that cold, terrifying place, Toad was led past the hangman's scaffold and the thumbscrew chamber to the grimmest dungeon imaginable.

The jailor selected the correct key from a great bunch he wore around his waist and then invited Toad to take up his new residence. Toad entered the dark dungeon and heard the door clang shut behind him. He was now a helpless prisoner in the remotest dungeon of the best-guarded prison of the stoutest castle to be found in the length and breadth of Merry England.

Toad knew that the grim darkness of an ancient fortress lay between him and the outer wall of sunshine, and a wonderful world of motor cars and gypsy caravans. He flung himself to the floor and started to cry the most bitter of tears.

"This is the end of everything," he wept. "At least, it is the end of the career of Toad. The

He was now a helpless prisoner.

popular, handsome, rich and hospitable Toad is no more. Once so carefree, will I ever be freed to travel the riverbank again? Will I stay here until people who were once proud to call me a friend forget the very name of Toad?

"Oh, wise old Badger. Oh, clever intelligent Rat. Oh, sensible Mole. How right you were. You tried to save me from myself. You did your best, but I wouldn't listen. Oh how I wished I had taken your advice!"

The days passed and Toad became sadder and sadder, and thinner and thinner. He couldn't eat a thing and he couldn't stop crying. He was wasting away.

Chapter 13
The Jailor's Daughter

Now the jailor had a daughter, a pleasant and good-hearted girl who helped her father in the prison. She was particularly fond of animals and besides her canary, she kept several mice and a squirrel.

This girl pitied poor Toad. "Father," she said one day, "I can't bear to see Toad so unhappy and getting so thin. Can I look after him? Can I make him my special prisoner? You know how fond of animals I am. I could feed him by hand."

Her father quickly agreed. So that day she went and knocked on Toad's dungeon door.

"Cheer up, Toad," she said. "Dry your eyes and try to eat something. Here, I've brought you some of my dinner."

It was bubble and squeak, a tasty dish of cabbage, carrot and potato. Its wonderful fragrance filled the cell.

Toad, lying silent on his bed of straw, immediately began to think that perhaps life was not so terrible after all. Bubble and squeak was one of his favorite dishes. However, he didn't stop crying, and he continued to sulk and moan about his lot. So the girl left him – but she didn't take the food with her.

The smell of the bubble and squeak reminded Toad of better times. He could not resist it and scoffed it down in seconds. Now he began to think new and inspiring thoughts; of chivalry, brave deeds, fine poetry and sunlit meadows, and bees buzzing in summer.

He began to think of his friends and how they would surely be able to do something to help him.

The girl returned at tea time with a nice cup of tea and buttered toast. The smell of that buttered toast simply talked to Toad. It talked of warm kitchens, breakfasts on bright frosty mornings and comfortable firesides with friends on winter evenings.

Toad sat up again, dried his eyes, sipped his tea and munched his toast. Soon he was talking to the girl about his house and what a lot his friends thought of him.

"Tell me more about Toad Hall," she said.

Bubble and squeak was one of his favorite dishes.

"Toad Hall is a very smart gentleman's residence, built in the fourteenth century," he replied proudly. "Yet it has every modern convenience now; up-to-date sanitation, five minutes from the church, post office and golf course."

"It sounds very nice," said the girl.

"Oh, it is," said Toad. "It has a boat house, a fish pond, a kitchen garden, pig pens, stables, pigeon and hen houses, a dairy, wash house and a banqueting hall. Oh what fun we have when all the animals are gathered together for a feast in the banqueting hall!"

The girl was enchanted by all that Toad told her. And she was delighted when Toad suddenly burst into a boastful song about Toad Hall. That night, Toad curled up on his straw bed and had the nicest of dreams.

In the following days, Toad and the girl had regular chats. She had become very fond of Toad and she thought it so unfair that he should be locked up for what seemed to her to be a very minor offence.

One day she came to his cell and spoke in a very secretive way. "Now listen to me," she said, almost in a whisper. "I have an aunt who is a washerwoman. She comes to the prison

She was enchanted by all that Toad told her.

once a week on a Monday and takes home the dirty washing."

"What's a washerwoman to me," said Toad, who was regaining some of his old confidence. "I don't normally talk to washerwomen. They are beneath me in the social way of things."

"Do be quiet a minute," said the girl. "You talk too much. That's your chief fault. Now listen. You're very rich, so you tell me very often. I believe if you offered my aunt some money, she might let you have her dress and bonnet."

"What on earth would I want a dress for?" cried Toad.

"To help you get out of here," said the girl. "She could let you have her dress and bonnet, and you could escape by pretending you were the washerwoman. Her dress would fit you, I'm sure. You have a similar figure to her."

"I assure you," said Toad in a huff, "that I have a very different figure from anyone else's. Mine is most elegant. And, look here, surely you wouldn't have Mr. Toad of Toad Hall running about the country disguised as a washerwoman!"

Toad's arrogance was too much for the girl. "Have it your own way," she said angrily. "I was only trying to help you. You're a horrid, proud and ungrateful animal. I suppose you want me to hire a coach and four horses for your escape!"

Chapter 14
Toad in Disguise

Toad was always ready to admit he was in the wrong. "I'm sorry," he said to the girl. "You're a good and kind little thing, and I am indeed a proud and stupid toad. Please introduce me to your worthy aunt, if you will be so kind. And I'm sure that the excellent lady and I will be able to agree financial terms."

The following evening, the girl ushered her aunt into Toad's dungeon. She immediately saw the line of gold coins that Toad had laid out in readiness. The financial arrangements were quickly agreed.

In return for the cash, Toad received a cotton dress, an apron, a shawl and a black bonnet. The aunt only asked for one more thing. She wanted to be gagged and tied up. That way no one would be suspicious of her part in Toad's escape.

Toad was delighted to oblige. It would enable him to leave the prison with some style, and a reputation for being a desperate and dangerous fellow.

Toad was quickly dressed in his washer-woman's clothes.

"Now hurry," said the girl. "Take the main stairs to the ground floor then go right to the main gate. The guards should let you straight through."

With a quaking heart, Toad set forth cautiously on what seemed to be a most hazardous journey to freedom. With his head down and a pile of washing under his arm, he walked quickly up the stone steps to reach the ground floor, passing many a guard on the way. He just waved politely and hurried on.

It seemed hours before he reached the main gate. The guard opened it as he approached. Toad was sure that his disguise would be spotted but the next moment, he was waved though. He found himself in the town's main street.

Now his first thought was of how to get home. The sound of a train whistling in the distance gave him his solution. He ran towards the railway station and joined the queue of people waiting to buy tickets.

At last it was Toad's turn. Suddenly he found himself in a great mess, trying to find his money. His hands eventually found their way through the washerwoman's dress.

But it was no use. He realized that he was no longer wearing his waistcoat beneath the dress. There were no pockets to be found and no money, either.

There was only one hope left. Speaking in his most educated and upper class voice, he spoke to the ticket clerk. "Look here, my dear boy," he said. "I have left my purse behind. Just give me the ticket and I will send the money tomorrow. I'm well-known in these parts."

The clerk stared at Toad and his black bonnet. "I should think you are pretty well-known in these parts if you've played this game of trying to get free tickets before," he said. "I don't believe you. Now move along. Next customer, please!"

In despair, Toad left the booking office and wandered up the platform. The train was already in the station. He was desperate. Any moment his escape from jail would be discovered and search parties would be sent out.

As he thought about his desperate position, he began to cry again. Just then he was passing the locomotive and the engineer spotted him.

"What's the matter, washerwoman?" he

It seemed hours before he reached the main gate.

asked. "Why are you crying?"

"I'm just a poor washerwoman who's left her money at home," Toad sobbed. "They won't give me a ticket to get home."

"I'll tell you what," said the engineer. "This is dirty work and I could do with some washing being done. It's against all regulations, but I'll give to you free ride home in the locomotive in exchange for some washing."

Toad was delighted and scrambled up into the locomotive. The guard waved his flag and blew his whistle. The train moved out of the station.

Soon the train was racing through the countryside, getting ever-closer to Toad Hall. Toad was already planning what he would have for supper, when the engineer suddenly turned to him.

"It's strange," he said. "We are the last train on the line tonight. Yet I can see another right behind us."

At that moment, the moon came out from behind the clouds. Now both the engineer and Toad could see that they were being followed at speed by another train.

"It looks like they are chasing us," said the engineer. "They are gaining on us fast. And if I'm not mistaken, it's carrying policemen!"

The clerk stared at Toad.

Chapter 15
The Chase

Toad knew the game was up. He went on his knees and begged the engineer to save him.

"I confess," he said. "I am not a washer-woman. I'm Mr. Toad of Toad Hall. I have just escaped from prison by my daring and cleverness. If they catch me, I'll live on bread and water for the rest of my life, and never see myself freed from the chains they'll put on me."

"Tell me the truth," said the engineer. "What were you put in jail for?"

"It was nothing," said Toad. "I only borrowed a motor car while the owner was at lunch. I didn't mean to steal it."

The engineer looked very grave. "I fear you have been a very wicked Toad," he said. "But I don't hold with being ordered about by policemen. So cheer up, Toad. I'll do my best to help you."

With that, he piled on more coal. The

The Chase

Still the pursuers were gaining on them.

furnace roared and sparks flew. But still the pursuers were gaining on them.

"They're lighter than us," said the engineer. "They'll reach us eventually. I've got a plan though. There's a tunnel ahead with a wood just beyond it. They'll have to slow down before entering the tunnel. It's safety regulations. So I'll do the opposite. I'll speed up as we enter the tunnel and then slam on the brakes as we reach the wood. When I'm going slow enough, you can jump off!"

Once more the engineer piled on the coals and soon they raced into the tunnel. Two minutes later the train shot out the end, its brakes screaming as it suddenly slowed.

Toad waited for it to slow down enough and then jumped for his life. He tumbled down the embankment and rolled into the wood, unharmed.

A few moments later the pursuit train came slowly out of the tunnel.

Toad laughed for the first time since leaving the prison, as he saw the two trains disappear into the distance. But he soon stopped laughing when he came to consider that it was now very late and very dark. He was also very hungry and in a wood he did not recognize.

He set off into the wood, trying to distance himself from the railway. He kept hearing strange sounds. He was sure he was being followed. An owl whooshed past his ear and he jumped with fright.

At last, cold, hungry and tired out, he sought the shelter of a hollow tree. He made as comfortable a bed as he could from branches and leaves, and then settled in. He was exhausted and slept like a log.

Toad was woken by the rising sun pouring into his hollow tree. Sitting up, he rubbed his eyes and for a moment, wondered where he

An owl whooshed past his ear.

was. He looked around for the stone wall of his prison cell. Then, with a leap of the heart, he remembered everything – his escape, the train ride and his being pursued by his jailors. But the best thing he remembered was that he was free!

Free! The very word delighted him. He was warm from one end to the other at the thought of the jolly world outside; a world ready to serve him and play up to him, a world anxious to help him and keep his company, as it always had in days of old before misfortune fell upon him.

Toad shook himself and combed the dry leaves out of his hair with his fingers. Then he marched forth into the morning sun, hungry but hopeful. All the terrors of the day before had vanished.

He had the world all to himself that early summer morning. The dewy woodland was solitary and still. The green fields were his own to do with as he liked. The road, when he reached it, was so lonely it just seemed to be begging for company.

Chapter 16
Aboard the Barge

There was a canal beside the road, but there was no sign of a bridge across it. Toad decided to follow the road and the canal in a westerly direction.

"One thing's clear," he said to himself. "The road and the canal must be coming from somewhere and going to somewhere."

So he plodded on and very soon afterwards saw a horse walking up behind him, on a path beside the canal. It had ropes attached to its collar and was pulling a canal barge behind it.

With a pleasant swirl of quiet water at its front, the barge slid up alongside Toad. Its sole occupant was a stout woman wearing a sun bonnet. She was steering the boat with an arm on the tiller.

"A nice morning," she remarked to Toad.

"I dare say it is," said Toad, quickly remembering that he was still dressed as a washer-

The barge slid up alongside Toad.

woman and still on the run from the police. He had to make up a story.

"A fine morning for some," he said. "But not for those in sore trouble. My married daughter has just sent for me to come at once. One of her children is ill. So I've had to leave my business. I'm in the washing and laundry line, you know. I've also lost all my money and lost my way."

"And where might your daughter be living?" asked the woman.

"She lives near the river ma'am," said Toad. "Close to a fine house called Toad Hall that's somewhere around these parts. Perhaps you have heard of it?"

"Toad Hall! Why, I'm going that way myself," said the woman. "This canal joins the river some miles further on, a little above Toad Hall. Then it's just a short walk. Come along with me in the barge. I'll give you a lift."

She steered the boat to the bank and Toad jumped aboard. "Toad's good luck again," he murmured to himself. "I always come out on top."

"So you're in the washing business, eh?" said the woman, as the boat glided along the canal with the horse towing it from the foot-path. "And a very good business it is, too."

"Finest business in the whole country," replied Toad. "All the important ladies and gentlemen come to me. They wouldn't go to anyone else even if they were paid to. They know me and my work so well. You see, I understand my work thoroughly, and attend to it all myself."

Toad was enjoying making up his story. "Washing, ironing, starching shirts . . . everything's done under my own eye," he continued.

"But surely you don't do all that work yourself, ma'am?" asked the woman.

"Oh, I have girls to help," replied Toad. "Twenty girls or thereabouts, always at work. But I'm never so happy as when I actually have my own hands in the washtub. A real pleasure."

"What a bit of luck then," said the woman. "This is a regular bit of good fortune for both of us."

"Why, what do you mean?" asked Toad nervously.

"Well, look at me now," she replied. "I like washing just like you, but I have to steer the boat. Yet down below is a huge pile of washing to be done. And seeing that you like to wash so much, I expect it would be a pleasure for you to do it for me. That way I shall know that you are

Toad was enjoying making up his story.

enjoying the boat ride, instead of sitting idle beside me."

"Oh, I don't know," said Toad, desperately thinking of anything to get him out of washing all the woman's clothes. "I don't think I would be good enough to wash your clothes. I might spoil them. I'm more into gentlemen's things. Perhaps I could steer the boat while you do the washing."

"Let you steer?" said the woman, laughing. "It takes a lot of practice to steer a barge. Besides it's dull work and I want you to be happy. No, you shall do the washing that you are so fond of. And I'll stick to steering. Don't try and deprive me of giving you a treat!"

Toad was cornered. He looked for an escape from doing the washing. "What a dreadful thought," he said to himself. "The famous Mr. Toad, doing the washing!"

Chapter 17
Toad Does the Washing

There was no escape for Toad. He resigned himself to his fate and went and collected the wash tub, water, soap and dirty clothes. He had never seen such dirty clothes.

Into the tub they went. He scrubbed and rubbed them, and beat them and squeezed them. But after an hour, they were still dirty. His back had started to ache and his paws were all wrinkled.

Now, Toad was very proud of his paws. He muttered and cursed under his breath, saying things that perhaps a washerwoman shouldn't have said. Then he lost the soap for the fiftieth time. He was getting so angry!

A burst of laughter made him straighten himself up and look round. He saw that the woman had been watching him and was laughing out aloud.

"I've been watching you all the time," she said. "I suspected as much. You never were a washerwoman, were you? I could tell by the puffed up way you talked. You've never washed a sock in your life."

Toad's temper, which had been simmering for some time, now boiled over. He lost control of himself.

"You common, lowdown, fat woman," he shouted. "Don't you dare talk to your betters like that! Washerwoman indeed! I would have you know that I am Toad, a very well-known, respected and distinguished Toad. I may be under a cloud at the moment, but I will not be laughed at by you!"

The woman moved closer and peered under his bonnet. "Why, so you are," she cried. "Well, I never! A horrid, nasty, crawly Toad. And in my nice clean barge – now that is a thing I will not have."

She left the tiller for a moment and caught hold of Toad, her right hand grabbing his left leg, her left hand his right. Then she threw him overboard.

Toad's world turned upside-down and he found himself flying through the air, revolving rapidly as he went. The water, when he eventually reached it with a loud splash, proved quite cold enough for his taste. However, its chill was

Toad Does the Washing

Toad scrubbed and rubbed the clothes.

not enough to quell his proud spirit or the heat of his furious temper.

Toad rose to the surface, spluttering. When he had wiped the weeds from his face, he looked up to see the woman still laughing at him. As he coughed and spluttered, he vowed to have his revenge on her.

He struck out for the shore, but his dress greatly slowed him down. When at last he reached the bank, he was out of breath. He rested for a moment or two and then, gathering up his wet skirts, started to run after the barge as fast as his legs would carry him. He was wild with indignation and thirsting for revenge.

The woman was still laughing when Toad finally drew level with her again.

"You'll have to iron that dress now," she chuckled. "But perhaps you should wash it first."

Toad never paused to reply. Solid revenge was what he wanted, not cheap words. And he had seen what he wanted just a little way upstream. Running swiftly, he overtook the horse that was towing the boat and quickly unfastened the ropes.

Then he leapt onto the horse and galloped off. Toad steered the horse for open country,

Running after the barge

abandoning the path altogether. But he had time to glance back and saw that the barge, now out of control, had crashed into the side of the canal.

The woman was screaming, shouting and wildly waving her arms. "Stop! Stop!" she shouted. "Bring that horse back immediately. I'll call the police."

But now it was Toad's turn to laugh. He had quite recovered his temper now that he had done something that he thought was very clever.

Soon after, Toad saw a gypsy caravan close by. A man was sitting on the steps outside, watching his breakfast cooking on a fire. Delicious smells wafted past Toad's nose. He was so hungry.

The man looked up and saw the horse. "Do you want to sell that horse of yours?" he asked.

It had not occurred to Toad that he might turn the horse into cash, and the cash into food. But now he thought it might be a good idea . . .

Chapter 18
Toad Makes a Bargain

"What?" cried Toad, pretending to be shocked by the man's offer. "Sell my beautiful horse? No! It's out of the question. How would I take my washing home? How would I get it back to my customers? Besides, I'm too fond of my horse. I love him and he loves me."

"Try and love a donkey instead," said the man. "Some people do."

"You don't seem to see," said Toad, "that my horse comes from a well-bred family. He's an aristocratic horse. He's a gentleman's horse. And he would be too expensive for you to buy."

"How about a shilling a leg?" suggested the man.

"A shilling a leg?" said Toad. "I would have to take a little time to work out exactly how much that would be."

Toad dismounted and did several sums with his fingers. "A shilling a leg," he announced after some long calculations, "would be four shillings. Oh no. That's far too little. I couldn't part with him for that."

"Well, I'll tell you what," said the man. "I'll make it five shillings in all. And that's my last word."

To a toad like Toad, five shillings might have appeared to be a large sum of money. On the other hand, it did not seem very much money for a horse. But then again, the horse hadn't cost him anything, so whatever he got was all profit.

At last Toad delivered his verdict. "Well, this is *my* last word," he said. "You can give me six shillings cash and as much breakfast as I can eat. In return, you shall have my horse and its harness. And if that's not good enough for you, then I'll be on my way."

The man declared he would be ruined if he did such a deal, but immediately handed over six shillings and offered Toad a seat by the fire.

As far as Toad was concerned, it was the tastiest breakfast he'd ever eaten. It was so good that he ate and ate until the pot was empty.

Afterwards, the man gave Toad directions to find his way home. He set off in a happy and contended mood. The sun was still shining, his

Toad Makes a Bargain

"How about a shilling a leg?"

The tastiest breakfast he'd ever eaten.

clothes were dry again and he was nearing home and friends, and safety.

As Toad walked along, he thought about all his adventures and escapes; and how when things seemed worst, he had always managed to find a way out. His pride began to swell again.

"Ho! Ho!" he cried. "What a clever Toad I am! There is no animal equal to me for cleverness in the whole world! My enemies shut me up in prison, with guards everywhere. And I just walked out. They pursued me and I just vanished into space. I might have been fooled for a while by the woman on the barge, but I got the better of her in the end."

He became so conceited at what he had done that he composed a song as he went along.

The world has held great heroes,
As history books have showed;
But never a name to go down to fame,
Compared with that of Toad.

The clever men at Oxford
Know all there is to be knowed.
But they none of them know one half as
much
As intelligent Mr. Toad.

The Queen and her Ladies-in-Waiting
Sat at the window and sewed.
She cried, "Look! Who's that handsome
man?"
They answered, "Mr. Toad."

Toad sang as he walked, his sense of pride growing all the time. There were many more verses he sang about himself but it would be

Toad sang as he walked.

terribly boastful to write any of them down. However, his pride was soon to have a great fall . . .

After some miles, Toad reached a main road again. He looked to the right and saw a speck approaching him. The speck turned into a dot. The dot turned into a blob and then into something very familiar – a motor car!

"Now this is more like it," said Toad. "The owner of the car will give me a lift. I might even end up by being driven right into Toad Hall in the car. That would be one in the eye for Badger!"

Toad stepped confidently into the road to hail the motor car. The vehicle was going at a gentle pace and slowed right down as it came close to Toad.

Toad suddenly went very pale. His stomach turned to water. His knees shook and his legs gave way. He collapsed to the ground. And well he might. The motor car was the very one he had stolen on the fatal day when all his troubles began!

Chapter 19
Behind the Wheel Again

"It's all over!" cried Toad, on seeing the familiar motor car. "Chains and policemen again! Prison again! Dry bread and water again! Oh, what a fool I have been. Why did I have to go strutting around the countryside, singing boastful songs about myself? Why didn't I just lay low till nightfall and then slip quietly home without any fuss. Oh, hapless Toad. Oh, ill-fated animal!"

The terrible motor car drew slowly nearer and nearer, till at last he heard it stop in front of him. Toad, not knowing what to do, slumped to the ground and played dead.

Two gentlemen got out and walked round the trembling heap of crumpled misery lying on the road.

"Oh dear, this is very sad," said one. "A washerwoman seems to have fainted. Perhaps she was overcome by heat. Possibly she's starving. Let's lift her into the car and take her to the nearest village, where she probably has friends."

They tenderly lifted Toad into the motor car, propped him up with cushions and proceeded on their way.

When Toad heard the gentlemen talk in such a kind and sympathetic manner, he knew that they had not recognized him as the creature that stole the car. His courage began to revive. He cautiously opened one eye, and then the other.

"Look!" said one of the gentlemen. "She is better already. The fresh air is doing her good. How do you feel now, ma'am?"

"Thank you kindly, sir," said Toad in a feeble voice. "I'm feeling a great deal better."

"That's good," said the gentleman. "Now keep quite still, and above all, don't try to talk. Just rest."

"I can't," replied Toad. "But I might, if only I could sit on the front seat beside the driver. There I could get the fresh air full in my face. I should soon be all right again."

"What a sensible woman," said the gentleman. "Of course you can."

The two men helped Toad into the front seat, and on they went once more.

Lifting Toad into the motor car

Toad was almost himself again. He sat up, looked about him and tried to do his best to hold down an ever growing desire to take control of the vehicle. But it was too strong for him.

"Please, sir," he said, "would you let me drive the car for a little way. I've been watching, and it looks so easy and so interesting. I should very much like to tell my friends that I have driven a motor car."

"Bravo!" cried one of the gentlemen. "I like your spirit, ma'am. We'll give you a try."

Toad eagerly clambered into the driving seat as the driver made space beside him. Toad took the steering wheel and listened to the instructions given, pretending he knew very little about driving.

Then he set the motor car in motion. He went very slowly at first, for he was determined to be careful after all that had happened in the past.

The gentlemen clapped their hands and applauded him. Toad heard one of them say, "How well she does it. Fancy a washerwoman driving a car as well as this!"

Toad went a little faster; then faster still, and even faster. He heard the gentlemen calling out, "Be careful, washerwoman!"

But sadly, Toad was not one to take orders.

He became quite angry at being told to go carefully. So he went even faster.

The man who had been driving tried to slow Toad by moving the brake. But now Toad's blood was up. The rush of air to his face, the hum of the engine and the jumping of the car beneath him gave him an irresistible thrill.

"Washerwoman indeed!" he cried. "Ho, ho! I am Toad, the motor car snatcher, the prison breaker, the Toad who always escapes. Sit still gentlemen, and you will know what driving is really about; for you are in the hands of the famous, the skilful, the entirely fearless Toad!"

With a cry of horror, the two gentlemen rose up and flung themselves on Toad.

"Seize him!" they cried. "Seize the wicked animal who stole our car! Drag him to the nearest police station! Down with the desperate and dangerous Toad!"

Alas! The gentlemen should have realized it might have been safer to stop the car before trying to arrest Toad. With a half-turn of the steering wheel, Toad sent the car crashing through a hedge. A mighty bound and a violent shock took the two gentlemen and the car into a muddy pond.

Toad himself was catapulted out of the car.

Toad went a little faster, then faster still.

Chapter 20
A Tumble into Deep Water

Toad found himself flying through the air, a little like a swallow in summer, swooping here and there. He quite liked the feeling and was beginning to wonder whether it would go on until he developed wings and became a Toad Bird. But then he began to sink. He landed on his back with a thump, in a meadow.

Sitting up, he could just see the motor car in the pond. It was almost submerged. The two gentlemen were floundering around in the murky pond water beside it.

Toad rapidly picked himself up and ran off across the countryside, as fast as he could, scrambling through hedges, jumping ditches and pounding across fields. Soon he was utterly breathless and weary. He slowed down to a gentle walk.

When Toad had recovered and was able to think calmly, he began to giggle. Then he was laughing so much he had to sit down again.

A Tumble into Deep Water

He landed on his back with a thump.

"Ho, ho!" he roared. "It's Toad again. He has come out on top once more. Who was it who got the men to give him a lift? Who managed to get into the front seat, for the sake of fresh air? Who persuaded them into letting him drive? Who landed them in the pond? Who escaped by flying through the air? Why Toad, of course. Clever Toad. Great Toad. Good Toad!"

Then he burst into song again.

The motor car went poop-poop-poop,
As it raced along the road.
Who was it steered it into a pond?
Ingenious Mr. Toad!

"Oh how clever I am!" cried Toad. "How clever! How clever! How clev . . ."

His words were cut short by a noise in the distance. Oh horror! Oh misery! Oh despair!

About two fields away, the two gentlemen were running towards Toad. And beside them were two policemen. They had seen him, possibly even heard him singing his own praises. And now they were on his tail.

Poor Toad sprang to his feet and raced away again, his heart in his mouth.

"Oh my!" he gasped. "What a boastful fool

I am. Swaggering again. Shouting and singing songs again. Oh my, oh my, oh my!"

Toad glanced back and saw to his dismay that they were gaining on him. On he ran desperately, but they were still catching him up. He did his best, but he was a fat little animal and his legs were short. He could hear them close behind now.

Ceasing to look where he was going, he struggled on blindly and wildly. Suddenly, he felt the earth vanish beneath his feet. He tumbled into deep water. It bore him away with such speed and force that he could not fight against it.

It was some moments before Toad realized what had happened. In his blind panic to escape his pursuers, he had run straight into the river. He tried to grasp the reeds on the riverbank, to stop himself from being washed away. But the current was so strong that it tore them out of his hands.

"Oh, poor me!" cried Toad. "I'll never sing another boastful song. Never!"

Just then Toad went under the water, only to surface breathless and spluttering.

Ahead of him was a big, dark hole in the riverbank. As the river bore him past, he

Tumbling into deep water

reached out with a paw and caught hold of the edge.

Then slowly, with great difficulty, he drew himself up out of the water, till he was at last able to rest his elbows on the edge of the hole. There he remained for some minutes, puffing and panting. He was quite exhausted.

As Toad sighed and puffed and stared into the dark hole, some bright small thing twinkled in its depths. It was moving towards him and as it approached, a face gradually emerged from the darkness. And what a familiar face it was – small and brown, with whiskers, round ears and silky hair.

It was Water Rat!

Chapter 21
Toad Gets an Awful Shock

Rat put out a neat little brown paw, gripped Toad firmly by the scruff of his neck and gave a great pull. Slowly but surely a very water-logged Toad came up, until he was safely on the edge of the hole.

He was streaked with mud and weed, and water streamed off him. But he was happy and high-spirited now that he found himself once more in the house of an old friend. No longer did he have to act like a fugitive from justice. The thought of getting rid of the dreadful washerwoman's clothes delighted him.

"Oh, Ratty," he cried. "I've been through such times since I saw you last. You can't imagine what I've been through. Such trials! Such suffering! And all of them so nobly borne! Then such escapes, such disguises, all so cleverly planned and carried out by me.

"Been in prison – got out of it, of course. Been thrown in a canal – swam ashore. Stole a horse – sold him for a large sum of money. Humbugged everybody – made 'em do exactly what I wanted. Oh, I am a smart Toad and make no mistake! What do you think my last exploit was? Just let me tell you . . ."

"Toad," interrupted Rat, gravely and firmly, "you go upstairs at once and take off that old dress. Clean yourself up, put on some proper clothes and come down looking like a gentle-man again, if you can. I have never set eyes on a shabbier, bedraggled, disreputable looking object in my life. Now stop swaggering and be off! I'll have something to say to you later."

At first, Toad thought about arguing with Ratty. He'd had enough of being ordered about in prison. However, he had just caught sight of himself in the looking-glass in Rat's hallway. He took one glance at the dress and the black bonnet, and changed his mind. Very quickly and humbly, he went upstairs to Rat's dressing room.

Toad had a thorough wash and brush-up, changed his clothes and then stood in front of the mirror for a long time, contemplating his looks with pride and pleasure. "How people ever mistook me for a washerwoman, I will never know," he remarked to himself.

"Now stop swaggering and be off!"

Toad Gets an Awful Shock

By the time Toad came down, lunch was on the table. He was starving! His last meal had been breakfast with the man who bought his horse.

"Now, Toad," said Rat, "I don't want to upset you after all you've been through. But seriously, don't you see what a complete fool you've been making of yourself? On your own admission you've been handcuffed, imprisoned, starved, chased, terrified out of your life, insulted, jeered at and flung into a canal!

"Where's the amusement in that? Where does the fun come in? And all because you had to steal a motor car. You know, you've never had anything but trouble since you first set your eyes on a car. Why did you have to steal one? Why do you want to be a convict?

"Do you suppose it gives me any pleasure, for instance, to hear other animals whispering behind my back that I'm the chap that keeps company with jailbirds?"

Now, it was a very comforting point in Toad's character that he was truly a very good-hearted animal and never minded being told off by his real friends. And it must be said, he could always see the other side of an argument.

"Quite right, my boy," said Toad. "I have

been a conceited idiot. From now on I'm going to be such a good Toad. As for motor cars, I've not been that keen on them since I almost got a ducking in the pond."

Ratty was pleased to hear it. But Toad hadn't finished talking. "And to prove that I can live without cars," he said, "I have had an idea – a really brilliant idea connected with motor boats."

"Forget it!" cried Rat. "You are banned from driving anything fast from now on!"

"Don't worry, Ratty. It was only an idea. We won't talk any more about it," Toad quickly agreed, seeing that his friend was becoming very angry.

Toad then announced that he was going home. "I shall stroll gently back to Toad Hall. I've had enough adventures," he said. "I shall in future lead a quiet, steady life, pottering around my property and improving it. There'll always be a bit of dinner for my friends when they come around.

"I shall keep a pony and trap to jog around the country, just like I did when I was young, in the good old days before I got restless and went in search of adventure."

"Stroll gently back to Toad Hall!" exclaimed

"I have been a conceited idiot."

Rat. "What are you talking about? Haven't you heard?"

"Heard what?" asked Toad, turning rather pale. "Go on, Ratty. Don't spare me. What has happened?"

"Do you mean to tell me," asked Ratty, "that you haven't been told about the stoats, weasels and ferrets?"

"What, the Wild Wooders?" cried Toad "What have they been up to?"

"They've taken over Toad Hall," announced Ratty.

Chapter 22
Stoats, Weasels and Ferrets

Toad leaned his elbows on the table, his chin on his paws. A large tear had welled up in each of his eyes. "Go on, Ratty," he said sadly, but heroically. "Tell me all. I can take it."

"When you stole the motor car, you disappeared from polite society," began Rat. "In short, you became a jailbird."

Toad merely nodded.

"Well, your descent into criminality was talked about a great deal down here," Rat continued. "Not just along the riverbank. But also in the Wild Wood. The Riverbankers stuck up for you. They said you had been badly treated and that there was no justice in the land any more.

"However, the animals of the Wild Wood said it served you right, and that it was time this sort of thing was stopped. And Wild Wooders like the stoats, weasels and ferrets got very cocky. They went around telling everyone that you'd never be allowed to return here."

Toad nodded again without saying a word.

"Mole and Badger stuck by you all along," said Rat. "They said you'd come back soon. They even moved into Toad Hall to keep it aired and ready for your return. Then one dark night a band of weasels, armed to the teeth, crept silently up the track to the hall. Simultaneously, a group of skirmishing stoats attacked from the side."

"What happened?" asked Toad anxiously.

"Well, Mole and Badger were sitting by the fire telling stories to each other, suspecting nothing. Suddenly those bloodthirsty villains burst into the hall and rushed in on the two of them.

"They made the best fight of it, but what was the use? They were unarmed and taken by surprise. And what good can two animals do against hundreds? The invaders took them, beat them with sticks and threw them out into the cold and wet. And the Wild Wooders have been living in Toad Hall ever since."

"It's disgraceful!" cried Toad.

"It is," replied Rat. "They lie in bed half the day and breakfast at all hours. The place is in a complete mess. It's not fit to be seen. They've been eating all your food and making bad jokes about you. They keep singing songs about you too; about the police, prison and stolen motor cars. They've told the mailman to redirect all their mail to the hall, because they've come to stay for good."

"Oh, have they?" shouted Toad, getting up and seizing a stick. "I'll jolly soon see about that!"

"It's no good," Rat called after him. "Come back! You'll only get into more trouble."

But Toad was off, and there was no holding him back. He marched rapidly down the road, his stick over his shoulder. He was fuming and muttering things to himself.

He didn't stop until he got to the front gates of Toad Hall.

Suddenly, out popped a long yellow ferret with a gun. "Who goes there?" the creature growled.

"Stuff and nonsense," replied Toad angrily. "What do you mean by talking to me like that? Come out here at once, or I'll . . ."

The ferret never said a word, but brought the gun to his shoulder. Toad wisely dropped to the ground. Bang! A bullet whistled over his head. Startled, Toad scrambled to his feet and

Toad angrily seized a stick

scampered off back down the road. He heard the ferret laughing after him.

Toad returned to Rat and told him what had happened.

"What did I tell you?" said Rat. "It's no good. They've got sentries posted everywhere. And they are all armed."

But Toad was not inclined to give up there and then. He borrowed Rat's boat and rowed around to where the front garden of Toad Hall rolled down to the riverbank.

Arriving within sight of his old home, he rested the oars and examined the lie of the

Scampering off back down the road

land. All seemed quiet. He could see the front of Toad Hall glowing in the evening sun, and the pigeons cooing on the roof. The garden was ablaze with colorful flowers.

Toad decided that he would row around to the boathouse. But he had only just got beneath the bridge over the river when a great stone dropped from above. It smashed through the bottom of the boat, which suddenly started to fill with water. It sank very quickly and Toad found himself struggling in the water.

Looking up, he saw two stoats leaning over the parapet of the bridge and laughing at him.

"It'll be your head next, Toady," one called out.

The indignant Toad swam to the shore and wearily returned to Rat's place, and revealed what had happened.

"I warned you, Toad," Rat sighed. "And now you've lost me my boat. I was so fond of that boat. You've also ruined the clothes that I lent you!"

Toad apologized. "I have been a headstrong Toad again," he said. "I will be humble and submissive in future, I promise. I will not do anything else without your kind advice and full approval."

The boat started to fill with water.

"If that is so," said Rat, "then my advice to you is to sit down with me and have some supper."

Chapter 23
Planning the War

Over supper, Toad and Rat planned what they were to do next.

"We can't do much until we have talked with Mole and Badger," said Rat. "We need to hold a conference to plan things."

Mole and Badger arrived soon after. "Welcome home, Toad," said Badger, before realizing what he had just said. "What am I saying? Home, indeed! Poor unhappy Toad. Poor homeless Toad."

Mole was delighted to see his old friend. "Hooray for old Toad!" he cried. "We thought we would never see you again. You must have been so clever to escape from jail."

Ratty tried to stop Toad from answering, but it was too late.

"Oh yes," Toad replied, "it was very clever of me. I also captured a railway train . . . "

He was about to go on and list all his adventures, but he saw Ratty looking at him seriously. "Actually," he confessed, "I've been a fool, as I'm sure you and Badger will see."

"Never mind," said Mole. "We've got very serious business to attend to. The position's about as bad as it could get – sentries all around Toad Hall, guns poking out everywhere, stones thrown at us whenever we move. But do you know the most annoying thing? It's how they keep laughing at us."

They talked long into the night and the conclusion was that it was much too dangerous to make a frontal attack on Toad Hall.

"Then it's all over," sobbed Toad. "I shall go and become a soldier and never see my beloved Toad Hall again."

"Cheer up," said the wise old Badger. "There are more ways of getting a place back than just trying to take it by storm. Now I'm going to tell you a secret."

Toad sat up and dried his eyes. Secrets had a great attraction for him, mainly because he couldn't keep them. He got a great thrill every time he learned of a secret, and then passed it on to someone else.

"There is an underground passage," said Badger, "that leads from the riverbank quite near here. And it leads right into Toad Hall."

"Hooray for old Toad!"

"Nonsense!" said Toad. "You've been listening to too many stories. There is no passage. I should know. I know every inch of Toad Hall and there's nothing of the sort, I assure you."

"My young friend," said Badger, "your father was a worthy animal and he was a particular friend of mine. He told me a great deal he wouldn't have dreamed of telling you. He discovered that passage and looked after it, and kept it clean. He thought it might come in handy one day. And he told me never to mention it to you."

"Why?" asked Toad.

"He said you couldn't keep a secret," replied Badger.

"Well," said Toad, "I am a bit of a talker, yes. A popular fellow such as I am has lots of friends. We do talk a lot amongst ourselves, witty stories and the like. And somehow my tongue always gets wagging. I have the gift of conversation. But never mind all that. How's this passage of yours going to help us?"

"Just listen," said Badger. "My spies tell me that there's going to be a big banquet in Toad Hall tomorrow night. It's the Chief Weasel's birthday. All the weasels will be gathered together in the dining hall. They will be eating,

"How's this passage of yours going to help?"

drinking and laughing, suspecting nothing. They won't even have their guns on them. They expect their guards to protect them."

"But the guards," said Toad. "How will we deal with them?"

"We won't need to deal with them," said Badger. "They are placed all around outside the building. And our tunnel comes up inside the pantry, right next to the banqueting hall."

"Aha!" cried Toad in delight. "Now I understand."

"So we shall creep out of the pantry," said Badger.

". . . with our pistols, swords and sticks," said Rat.

". . . and rush in on them," said Badger.

". . . and whack 'em and whack 'em, and whack 'em!" cried Toad, hopping up and down in excitement.

"Very well," said Badger. "So that's our plan. There's nothing more to argue about. Now off to bed everyone. We need to be well rested before we begin our mission. And tomorrow morning at breakfast, we will make our final plans."

Chapter 24
The Morning of the Attack

Toad was much too excited to go to sleep right away that night. But when he did eventually doze off, he dreamed of roads that ran away from him just when he wanted to walk on them, canals that chased and caught him and a barge that sailed into the banqueting hall at Toad Hall with the week's washing.

He slept in late the next morning. When he came down to breakfast, all the other animals had already finished eating. Mole had already slipped off by himself, telling no one where he was going.

Badger sat in a large armchair reading the newspaper, hardly giving a thought to what was to happen that evening. Rat, on the other hand, was busily running around the room with his arms full of weapons. He was distributing them in four heaps. As he did so, he spoke excitedly under his breath.

"Here's a sword for me, a sword for Mole,

one for Badger and another for Toad. Here's a pistol for me, a pistol for Mole, a pistol for Badger and a pistol for Toad."

And so on and so on, until the heaps were piled high.

"That's all very well, Ratty" said Badger, looking up over his newspaper. "But just let us get past the stoats with their guns, and we won't want swords or pistols. Once we're in the hall, we four will clear out the lot of them with just a stick each. In fact, I would do the whole job myself, but I wouldn't want to deprive you chaps of all the fun."

"It's better to be on the safe side," said Rat, polishing a pistol barrel on his sleeve.

Just then Mole returned. He came tumbling into the room, very pleased with himself. "I've been having such fun," he declared. "I've been making fun of the stoats."

"I hope you've been careful," said Rat.

"Oh, I was," laughed Mole. "I found Toad's washerwoman's dress. I put it on, together with the bonnet and shawl, and went off to Toad Hall, bold as you please. The stoat sentries were on the look-out, of course, and they came out with their guns. 'Good morning' says I, very politely. 'Do you want any washing done today?'

Distributing the weapons

"They looked at me rudely and told me to go away. But I persuaded them to have their trousers washed, and said they would have them back by this afternoon. They finally agreed. I've got them all in my bag. So if we fight them tonight, they'll be a little embarrassed without their trousers."

"You silly creature," said Toad very loftily.

The fact was that he felt exceedingly jealous of Mole. It was just the sort of thing he would have loved to have done, if he had thought of it first.

But Mole hadn't finished. "Their commander came out to see what was happening. I told him a good tale, too. I said that my daughter was washerwoman to Badger and she had overheard all our plans to recapture Toad Hall."

"I hope you didn't tell him anything, Mole," said Badger.

"Oh, I told him everything," laughed Mole. "I said a hundred bloodthirsty badgers, armed with rifles, would make the first frontal attack. Six boat loads of rats would come in by river. That would be followed by a regiment of die-hard or death-or-glory toads. I said they had better get out of the hall before the battle began."

Mole had told the commander a good tale.

"What happened next?" asked Rat.

"I walked off," said Mole, "but soon after, I stopped and crept back to see what they were doing. They were in a complete panic, rushing around and falling over each other, everyone giving orders to everyone else."

"Oh, you are a silly creature, Mole," shouted Toad. "You've gone and spoilt everything. They know we're going to attack now."

But Badger disagreed. "Mole," he said quietly, "you have more sense in your little finger than most animals have in their whole bodies. You have put great panic in the enemy's mind. That will help us enormously."

Toad was just too jealous to speak. Oh, how he wished he had stolen the stoats' trousers!

Chapter 25
Badger's Army

At lunch time, final preparations for the assault on Toad Hall were made. Everyone ate a big meal of bacon, broad beans and macaroni pudding.

Afterwards, Badger sat down in his armchair. "We'll have our work cut out for us tonight," he said. "It'll be late before we're quite through with it. So I'm just going to take forty winks while I can."

Badger pulled a large handkerchief over his face and was soon snoring away.

Rat, still anxious, resumed his preparations, adding more things to his four heaps of weapons and equipment.

Mole was nervous too, but he took Toad outside and made him recount every detail of his arrest, imprisonment and escape, just to pass the time. This time Toad had no one to check whether he was telling the truth all the time. He wildly exaggerated all his adventures, but Mole didn't mind.

As it began to grow dark, Rat summoned everyone to his parlor and made each of them stand to attention by one of the piles. Then he gave each animal his equipment.

First there was a belt, then one sword to stick into each belt, and then another sword on the other side, for balance. Then came a pair of pistols each, a large stick, several sets of hand-cuffs, bandages and sticking plaster for the wounded, a flask of water and a sandwich case.

Badger quietly put down his equipment. "Sorry, Ratty," he said, "this is all too much. I shall only be taking my stick."

But the others went fully armed.

When all was ready, Badger took a lantern in one paw and his big stick in the other. "Now follow me!" he cried. "And don't chatter, Toady. We need to be absolutely silent."

Badger led his little army along the river until they reached a place that was heavily overgrown. "Here's where the secret tunnel begins – follow me," he whispered, slipping down the bank.

Mole and Rat had no problems following Badger. But Toad managed to slip and fall into the river, with a loud splash and cry of alarm.

Toad wildly exaggerated all his adventures.

He was hauled out by his friends.

At last, they all found themselves in the secret tunnel. It was cold and damp, and low and narrow. Toad began to shiver, partly from dread of what lay ahead and partly because he was wet through. He kept falling behind.

"Come on, Toad," whispered Badger. "Catch up."

A terror of being left behind in the dark tunnel forced Toad to hurry on. Now he moved forward so quickly that he bumped into the other three, who thought they were being attacked from behind.

Badger was about to raise his stick to his attacker, when he saw it was Toad. "Toad!" he growled. "Another incident like that and I'll send you home!"

So they slowly shuffled on, with their ears pricked for any sound of the enemy. After a while, Badger spoke again. "We ought to be almost under Toad Hall by now."

Suddenly they heard the sound of voices, coming from above. They guessed that they were immediately beneath the banqueting hall. The passage now began to slope upwards and as they advanced, the noise of the party above them became louder and louder.

They found themselves in the secret tunnel.

"What a celebration they are having," said Badger.

The group finally came to a stop beneath a wooden trapdoor. Badger heaved it up. One by one, Badger's army emerged into the pantry. Only a single door now stood between them and the party guests.

Just then, someone made a loud banging sound on a table in the banqueting hall and the guests fell silent. It was the Chief Weasel and he was going to give his birthday speech.

"My dear friends," he laughed, "I think I should thank our kind host for allowing me to have a party here tonight. I am talking about Toad, of course. Once we knew him a Good Toad, Honorable Toad, Modest Toad."

There were lots of shrieks of laughter from the guests, before the Chief Weasel continued. "But today we know him as Foolish Toad, Convict Toad. Yet we must give him some credit for providing me with a new home and an excellent place for a birthday party."

Toad was furious when he heard what was being said about him. "Let me get at him!" he snarled.

"Hold on a moment," said Badger. "Get ready, all of you!"

Badger's army emerged into the pantry.

Then Badger drew himself to his full height, took a firm grip on his stick and glanced at his comrades.

"The hour has come!" he cried. "Follow me!"

Chapter 26
The Battle of Toad Hall

Badger flung the pantry door wide open and he burst into the crowded banqueting hall, with Rat, Toad and Mole. There might have been only four of them, but they shouted and screamed like four hundred.

The terrified weasels dived under the tables. The panic-stricken ferrets sprang madly up at the windows to escape, or rushed wildly for the fireplace and got hopelessly jammed in the chimney. In the panic of the moment, tables and chairs were overturned and glass and china sent crashing to the floor.

Our heroes strode gallantly into the center of the room ... the mighty Badger, his whiskers bristling, his stick whistling through the air. Mole, black and grim, brandishing his stick and shouting out his war cry, "A Mole! A Mole!"

Rat, desperate and determined, his belt bulging with weapons of all sorts. And Toad,

They burst into the crowded banqueting hall.

frenzied with excitement and leaping into the air, while shouting terrifying Toad-whoops that chilled the enemy to the bone.

As far as the Chief Weasel's guests were concerned, the hall seemed to be filled with hundreds of badgers, water rats, moles and toads, wielding hundreds of sticks against their backsides. They were in a complete and utter panic, racing out of the hall and escaping across the lawns, dashing anywhere to escape the sticks.

Toad attended personally to the Chief Weasel, sending him flying across the room with a tremendous blow from his stick. The battle was soon over without a pistol being fired or a sword thrust in anger. Now Mole and Ratty were busily engaged in fitting handcuffs to the villains of the piece.

The banqueting hall was cleared in five minutes.

"Mole," said Badger, "you're the best of fellows. The weasels are defeated. The ferrets have run for it. Now pop along and sort out those stoat sentries. We shan't have much trouble with them now."

Mole returned a little while later to report that the stoats had fled too, leaving all their weapons behind.

"Right," said Badger, "there are two things left to do. First, Rat, take some of the prisoners and make them clean the house from top to bottom. I want it nice and clean for Toad to move back into. And after that, seeing that the weasels left their feast behind, perhaps we should eat it for them."

Later, the gallant four sat down to eat the Chief Weasel's birthday banquet. At the end, Toad, feeling deeply humbled by his friends' help, made a short speech.

"How can I thank you enough for giving me back my home?" he said. "You risked your lives for me. You will always be welcome at my house."

Toad was about to finish, but he couldn't resist a small boast. "Did you see how I tumbled the Chief Weasel? Sent him flying, I did!"

"Yes indeed you did, brave Toad," said Badger.

That night they all slept very well but as usual, Toad was last down for breakfast. He found every scrap of food gone. Badger appeared and tapped Toad on the shoulder.

"You have work to do," he said.

"What work?"

"Now that you are back in your home," he said, "you must hold an official banquet and invite all your friends to celebrate. This morning you must write the invitations and send them out."

At first Toad was angry that he couldn't go and play with everyone else. But as he wrote the invitations, he had an idea. He would add to the invitations a list of speeches and songs to be performed by him during the banquet.

So he wrote down a list of entertainments on each invitation:

Main speech   *By Toad*

Further speeches will be given by Toad during the evening.

Main address   *By Toad*

Special Talk   *In which Toad will talk about the prison system, canals, horse-dealing, motor cars and how he defeated the Chief Weasel*

Songs   *All to be sung by Toad*

"You have work to do."

When the invitations were complete Toad gave them to a small weasel who had stayed on as his servant. He instructed the miserable creature to deliver them to all his friends . . .

Chapter 27
Toad's Banquet

In no time at all, Mole and Rat got word of Toad's plans. They went to visit him the next day.

"Now look here, Toad," said Rat. "We are not going to allow you to give speeches, talks and songs at the banquet. You will simply bore all your guests to death with your huge exaggerations and inventions."

"But couldn't I sing just one song and give one speech?" pleaded Toad.

"Not one!" said Mole firmly.

Toad thought for a while, and then agreed. "You are right," he said at last. "It is time I changed my ways. I must stop boasting. But what about the invitations? They have all been sent out. My guests will be expecting me to sing and give talks."

"No they won't," said Mole. "We caught the weasel before he could deliver a single one. We've burned them. So now you must sit down and write them all again."

"Oh no!" howled poor Toad, who had spent hours on the first invitations.

On the night of the banquet, Toad stood proudly at the main door of Toad Hall welcoming his guests. Everyone was only too pleased to congratulate him on his return to his home. And he seemed such a modest Toad now – not boastful at all. How they cheered him for helping to win the Battle of Toad Hall!

Toad answered their cheers in a most unexpected way. "I did nothing," he said. "Badger was the mastermind, Mole and Ratty did most of the fighting. I merely served in the ranks and did what I was told."

"How very unlike Toad not to boast," Rat whispered to Mole. "Perhaps he has changed his ways for good now."

And when the assembled crowd called for Toad to give a speech, he simply raised his hand to indicate he would not be saying a word that night.

Toad was indeed an altered Toad! Or so they thought . . .

***

How they cheered him!

In the days that followed, Toad bought a gold chain which he sent to the jailor's daughter as a thank-you for helping him to escape. He sent a sparkling five pound note to thank the driver of the locomotive who had helped him so much. Toad even sent money to the barge woman to pay for the horse he had stolen.

In later years, during long summer evenings, Badger, Mole, Rat and Toad would stroll together in the Wild Wood, talking of old times. The wood had been tamed now, thanks to Badger and his friends winning the war.

Mother weasels would bring out their young and point to the gentlemen, as they passed by. "Look, baby," they would say. "There goes the wise Mr. Badger and the great Mr. Toad. And that's the gallant Water Rat, a terrible fighter. And yonder comes the clever Mr. Mole. We'll never see the like of them again."

And other mothers would give their children a special warning. "Behave yourself or I'll ask the terrible Mr. Badger to come and get you! And if that doesn't work, I'll get Mr. Toad to come and boast to you until you beg for mercy."

It's true that Toad had become a changed creature. Yet sometimes, when he was all alone

Toad's Banquet

Strolling together in the Wild Wood

in the Wild Wood, he would sing one of his boasting songs.

His favorite was the Ballad of the Battle of Toad Hall.

The Toad came home!
There was panic in the parlor and howling in
the hall,
There was crying in the cowshed and
shrieking in the stall,
When the Toad came home!

When the Toad came home!
There was smashing in of window and
crashing in of door,
There was chivvying of weasels that fainted
on the floor.
When the Toad came home!

Bang! Go the drums!
The trumpeters are tooting and the soldiers
are saluting,
And the cannon they are shooting and the
motor cars are hooting,
As the Hero comes home!

Shout hoo-ray!
And let each one of the crowd try and shout
it very loud,
In honor of an animal of whom you're justly
proud,
For it's Toad's great day!

And all those who heard him smiled to themselves as they went about their business, living in peace and contentment in the Wild Wood.

The End